DISCARDED

For Mika and Yoshi
(with special thanks to Victoria,
Jackie, Chris, and Sara) —KM

For Matthew —CT

Library of Congress Cataloging-in-Publication Data

Names: Maclear, Kyo, 1970- author. | Turnham, Chris,
1966- illustrator. Title: Hello rain / by Kyo Maclear;
illustrated by Chris Turnham. Description: San Francisco :
Chronicle Books, [2021] | Audience: Ages 3-5. | Summary:
A young girl experiences a rain storm from seeing the storm
roll in, to splashing in the puddles, and then finally watching
the sun coming back out. Identifiers: LCCN 2020027360 |
ISBN 9781452138190 (hardcover). Subjects: CYAC: Rain and
rainfall—Fiction. Classification: LCC PZ7.M2246 He 2021 |
DDC [E]—dc23. LC record available at
https://lccn.loc.gov/2020027360

ISBN 978-1-4521-3819-0

Manufactured in China.

Design by Sara Gillingham Studio.
Typeset in Brandon and Futura BT.
The illustrations in this book were rendered digitally.

10 9 8 7 6 5 4 3 2

Chronicle Books LLC
680 Second Street
San Francisco, California 94107

Chronicle Books—we see things differently. 6/21
Become part of our community at www.chroniclekids.com.

Hello, Rain!

KYO MACLEAR + CHRIS TURNHAM

chronicle books · san francisco

The air is full of waiting.
The sky is full of breeze.
The trees gust and billow.
All before it rains.

Rumble, rumble.
Distant thunder.
Rain is coming,
rain is coming.

Plink,
   plunk,
      plonk

      on the rooftop.

         Drip drop,
            metal mailbox ping.

Every rainfall plays
a different tune.

Listen. Listen.

Rain.
Rain.
Rain.

Old raincoat,

rubber boots,

big umbrella, best umbrella:

green, orange, yellow, blue.

Let's go outside!

On the streets,
umbrellas bloom.

Around us,
a game of HURRY.

Dash,
dart.

Skitter,
scatter.

But, why hurry
when the sky
is an adventure?

Deluge,
downpour,

sprinkle,
storm,

a drizzle,
a mizzle.

So many words
for rain!

Long thin threads.
    Tiny parachutes.
Buckets at a time.

Out of many drops—
   One.

     Big—

Curbside waterfall.

Downhill swoosh.

Out of many drops—

One.
Rushing.
River.

Let's launch the fleet!

Drippy leaf,
slippy rock.

Here is an earthworm,
a sticky snail.

Here is a seedling.

Even when it pours
the frogs don't hurry

or hide.

Hyacinth, foxglove, poppy,

yarrow.

Down in the dirt,
the thirsty roots
are drinking.

Cool rain.
Fresh rain.

A barrel to catch
the drops for later.

So we can have:
pink roses,
frilly peonies,
tangles of vine.

Bursting peapods,
bright carrots,
leafy radishes.

Plums in the fridge,
sweet and cold.

One for you,
one for me.

In a quiet spot,
a single drop of rain
touches five times—

a branch,
            a leaf,
an apple,
            a rock,
a blade of grass—

before reaching
the ground.

We crouch under a tree
and whisper-talk until . . .

Crack!

Inside.
Wet socks.
Drippy pants.

Shake-shake-shake
of rain-drenched fur.

Inside.
    Dry and warm.
Rain trickle flows
        against the window.
Mini rivers,
        droplets joining,
moving down, down,
        side to side.

Wanna play a board game?

Wanna read a book?

Wanna build a fort?

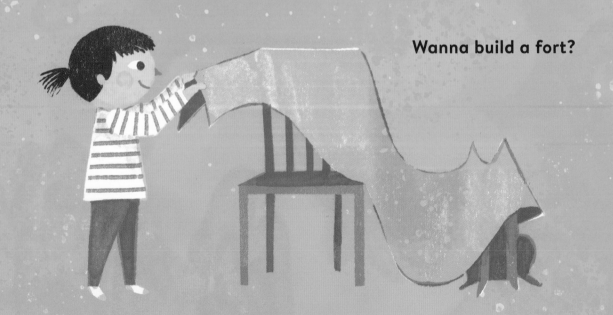

Naps and secrets
are both better—

when it rains.

I wonder
how the rain decides
how and when to be?

I wonder how it decides when to

plonk

. . . plunk

. . . plink

. . . stop?

The ground is glistening green.

Can you smell the grassy sweetness?

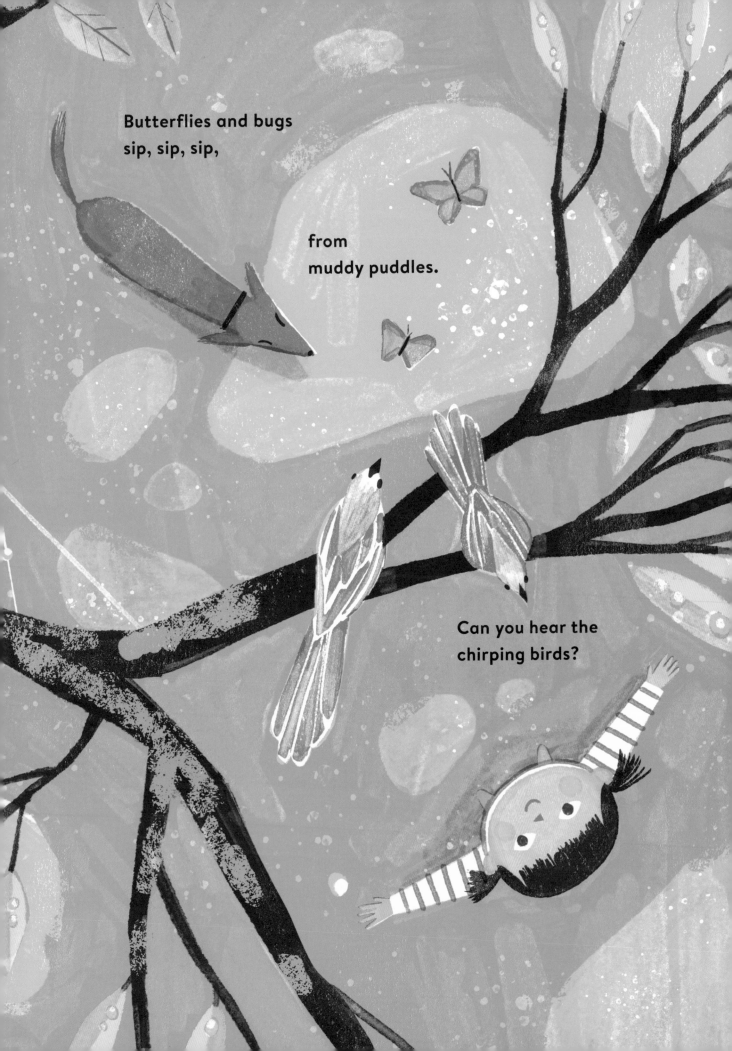

Butterflies and bugs
sip, sip, sip,

from
muddy puddles.

Can you hear the
chirping birds?

Hello, sparrows
    with your bright sparrow voices.
Hello, goldfinches
    with your *swee-swee* song.

Hello, flowers.
    Ripe and rosy.
Hello, mushrooms.
    Plump and proud.

Hello,
Sun!